How the Elephant got his Trunk

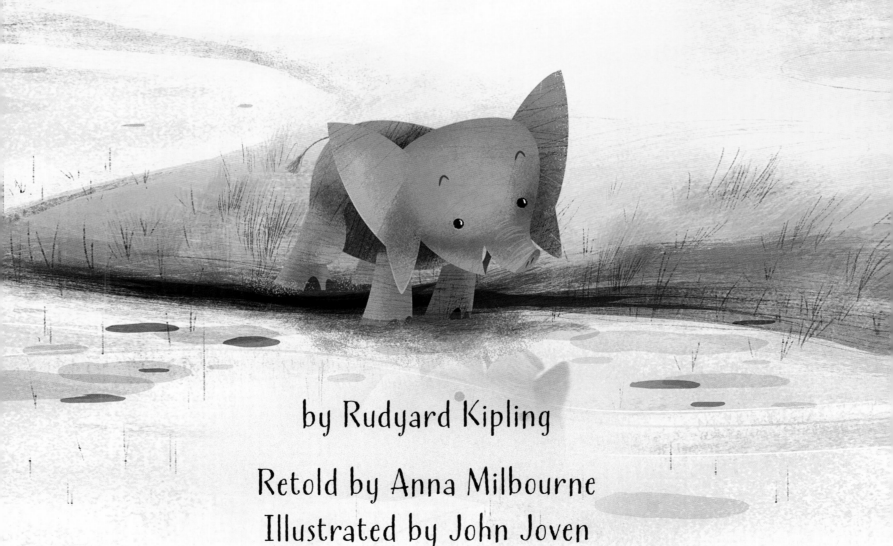

by Rudyard Kipling

Retold by Anna Milbourne

Illustrated by John Joven

Once, in a time long forgotten, elephants didn't
have trunks. They just had short, stumpy noses.

This story tells how those short,
stumpy noses became long.

Baby Elephant was very curious. He was always asking questions.
"Why does Ostrich have feathers?... Why does Giraffe have spots?"

One day he asked,
"What does Crocodile eat?"

"Hush, Baby Elephant!"
said his mother.

So Elephant went to see his friend Snake.
"What does Crocodile eat?" he asked.

"I don't know," Snake replied. "He lives in the great, green Limpopo River. Why not ask him yourself?"

Elephant went down to the great, green Limpopo River and found Crocodile basking in the shallows.

"Excuse me, Crocodile. What do you eat?" Elephant asked politely.

Crocodile smiled
a dangerous smile.

"Why, little Elephant,
don't you know?"

"I eat...

ELEPHANTS!"

With a quick snip-snap, Crocodile caught Elephant's nose.
"Let go!" squealed Elephant. But Crocodile did not let go.
He pulled and pulled as hard as he could.

"Oh dear," said Snake.

"Help!" cried Elephant.
"I'm slipping!"
A little white bird
caught hold of his tail.

Snake wound himself around Elephant's tummy. They pulled and pulled with all their might.

At last, Crocodile let go.

"Maybe I'll have fish today," he said, and slunk back into the river.

"Oh no," said Elephant. "Look!"
His nose had stretched!

It was a little sore
and very, very long!

"Don't worry," said Snake.
"A long nose might be useful."

Elephant's nose soon felt better.
And, to his surprise, he **did** find it useful!

With his new, long nose,
Elephant could
squirt water...

brush pesky flies away...

...and pick juicy fruit from tall trees.

Elephant went home happily and showed his family his new, long nose.

"Where did you get that?" everyone asked.

"Crocodile gave it to me,"
said Elephant.

When they saw how useful Baby Elephant's new, long nose was, all the others went down to the great, green Limpopo River...

...and got
long noses too!

How the Elephant got his Trunk is from the book
Just So Stories by Rudyard Kipling, which tells stories
of how animals came to be the way they are.

Edited by Lesley Sims
Designed by Sam Whibley

First published in 2016 by Usborne Publishing Ltd., Usborne House, 83-85 Saffron Hill,
London EC1N 8RT, England. www.usborne.com Copyright © 2016, 2015 Usborne Publishing Ltd.